CHILDREN'S THRIFT CLASSICS

Robinson Crusoe

DANIEL DEFOE

Adapted by
Bob Blaisdell

Illustrated by
John Green

DOVER PUBLICATIONS, INC.
New York

DOVER CHILDREN'S THRIFT CLASSICS
EDITOR OF THIS VOLUME: CANDACE WARD

Bibliographical Note

This Dover edition, first published in 1995, is a new abridgment of the work based on a standard text. The introductory Note and illustrations have been specially prepared for this edition.

Library of Congress Cataloging-in-Publication Data

Defoe, Daniel, 1661?–1731.
    Robinson Crusoe / Daniel Defoe ; abridged by Bob Blaisdell ; illustrated by John Green.
        p.   cm. — (Dover children's thrift classics)
    Summary: During one of his several adventurous voyages in the 1600s, an Englishman becomes the sole survivor of a shipwreck and lives for nearly thirty years on a deserted island.
    ISBN-13: 978-0-486-28816-1 (pbk.)
    ISBN-10: 0-486-28816-1 (pbk.)
    [1. Shipwrecks—Fiction.   2. Survival—Fiction.]   I. Blaisdell, Robert.
II. Green, John, 1948–   ill.   III. Title.   IV. Series.
PZ7.D36Ro   1995
[Fic]—dc20   95–36752
                                                                                CIP
                                                                                AC

Manufactured in the United States by RR Donnelley
28816107   2015
www.doverpublications.com

Note

DANIEL DEFOE (1661[?]–1731) was born in London. He was raised as a Nonconformist, or Dissenter, and since he could not attend Oxford or Cambridge because of his religious beliefs, he was educated at the Dissenters' academy at Newington Green. Defoe's first career was as a merchant, and he remained in trade for much of his adulthood. He began writing political pamphlets on economic, religious and other issues as early as 1683, but it wasn't until 1719 that Defoe wrote his first and most famous novel, *Robinson Crusoe*. Based on the adventures of the Scottish adventurer Alexander Selkirk, who was rescued in 1709 after being marooned on a desert island for five years, Defoe's novel first appeared as a true narrative. In its first year, the book went through three printings. Today, Robinson Crusoe remains one of literature's most fascinating fictional characters and his story remains a literary classic for children and adults.

This edition, specially adapted by Bob Blaisdell, retains all the excitement of the original, while condensing Defoe's text especially for young readers.

Contents

List of Illustrations

1
I Go to Sea

I WAS BORN in the year 1632, in the city of York, England, of a good family. My parents named me Robinson Crusoe. I had two older brothers, one of whom was killed in a war. What happened to my second brother I never knew, any more than my father or mother later knew what happened to me.

My father, who was a merchant and very old, had given me a good education, and wanted me to become a lawyer. I, however, would be happy with nothing but becoming a sailor, and so my father called me one morning into his room, and lectured me very harshly about my seafaring desires. Then he said that he would do very kind things for me if I would stay and settle at home. To close all, he told me I had my older brother for an example, to whom he had used the same arguments to keep him from going to war. My brother, instead, had entered the army and was killed.

When he mentioned my brother's fate, I saw the tears run down his face, and then he broke off his lecture, saying he was so sad he could no longer speak to me.

In spite of my father's wishes, I decided, a few

weeks after, to run away. But first I told my mother that I was determined to do so; that I was now eighteen years old; and if she would speak to my father to let me go on one voyage, and I did not like it, I would go no more, and I would promise to work doubly hard to regain the time I had lost.

She said there was no sense speaking to my father; and that, if I wanted to ruin myself, there was no help for it; they would never give their consent to such a plan.

It was not till almost a year after this that I broke loose. One day a friend, who was about to go to sea to London in his father's ship, encouraged me to go with them. I agreed to do so. I did not inform my parents. And so, on the first of September, 1651, I went on board a ship bound for London. The ship was no sooner out of the port but the wind began to blow, and the sea to rise in a most frightful manner. As I had never been at sea before, I was very sick. I decided if I ever got my foot upon dry land again, I would go directly home to my father and never set it into a ship again.

These thoughts continued all during the storm; but the next day the wind died down and the sea was calmer, and I began to get used to it. Towards night the weather cleared up, and a fine evening followed; the sun went down perfectly clear, and rose so the next morning. I entirely forgot the decision I had made in my distress to return to my father and give up the sea.

My friend's father, when I met him soon after, scolded me when he heard of my father's protests against my going on a ship. "Young man," said he, "depend upon it, if you do not go back, wherever you go, you will meet with nothing but disasters and disappointments, till your father's warnings come true."

I refused to go home. I disliked the idea of being laughed at by my neighbors for being turned back so quickly by the sea. In London I went on board a vessel bound to the coast of Africa.

This was the only voyage which I may say was successful in all my adventures, and which I owe to the captain, who taught me mathematics and the rules of navigation—things that were necessary to be understood by a sailor.

On my next voyage I fell into terrible misfortunes. Our ship was making her course towards the Canary Islands, and we were surprised in the gray of morning by a Turkish pirate ship. They chased us for several hours. They caught us and boarded our ship, killing a few of our men and wounding several others, and so we had to surrender. We were carried as prisoners into a Moorish port.

I was kept by the captain of the pirate ship and made his slave. When he went back to sea, he left me on shore to look after his little garden and do the common work around his house. When he came home again from his cruise, he ordered me to sit in the ship cabin to safeguard his vessel.

For two years, though I often tried to think of a way to escape, I found no help to do so. But then, after my master got used to sending me out in a small boat to do his fishing for him, I and one of his Moorish servant boys made our getaway in this boat. "Xury," I told the boy, "if you will be faithful to me, I'll make you a great man." Xury swore to be faithful to me and to go all over the world with me. For five days, as we were well-supplied with food, I would not stop or go on shore.

Finally, I ventured to the coast and put out our anchor in the mouth of a little river. I neither saw, or desired to see, any people; the main thing I wanted was fresh water. Xury said if I would let him go on shore with one of the empty water jars, he would find if there was any water and bring some to me. I asked him, "Why should not I go, and you stay in the boat?" The boy answered, "If wild mans come, they eat me, and you get away."

"Well, Xury," I said, "we will both go, and if the wild mans come, we will kill them; they shall eat neither of us." We hauled the boat in near the shore, and waded onto shore, carrying nothing but our guns and two jars for water.

A little higher up the creek, we found the water fresh when the tide was out, which flows but a little way up. So we filled our jars and feasted on a rabbit we had caught, and went on our way, having seen no footsteps of any human creature.

Several times I was obliged to land for fresh water

after we had left this place. We went southward for many days, living very tightly on our food. My plan was to get to the river Gambia or Senegal, anywhere close to Cape Verde, where I was in hopes to meet with some European ship.

One day, as we came within sight of the Cape Verge islands, Xury cried out, "Master, master, a ship with a sail!"

I jumped out of the cabin and immediately saw a Portuguese ship. With all the sail power I could make, I found we would not be able to cross their path and that they would be gone before I could make any signal to them. But they, it seems, saw me by the help of a spyglass and lay in wait for me to catch up.

I immediately offered all I had to the captain of the ship as a return for my rescue. He generously told me he would take nothing from me, that all I had would be delivered safe to me when I came to Brazil. "I will carry you there, Mr. Englishman," he said, "and those things will help you to buy your food and lodging and your passage home again."

He offered me a sack of money for my boy Xury, which I did not want to take. I did not want to sell the poor boy's liberty after he had helped me so well in gaining my own. When I let the captain hear my reason, he suggested a compromise, that he would give the boy his freedom after ten years. With this, and Xury saying he was willing to go to him, I let the captain have him.

We had a very good voyage to Brazil and arrived in

All Saints' Bay about twenty-two days after. I had not been long here before I met a good honest man who owned a plantation and sugar house. Seeing how well the planters lived and how they grew rich suddenly, I decided I would become a planter myself.

But alas! for me to do wrong that never did right was no great wonder. I was a planter for three years and discovered that I was doing what I did not enjoy. I might as well have stayed at home and never have tired myself in the world as I had done. And I used often to say to myself, I could have done this as well in England among my friends as have gone five thousand miles off to do it among strangers and savages in a wilderness.

I had nobody to talk with but now and then a neighbor. All the work that had to be done, I had to do it. I used to say I lived just like a man cast away upon some desolate island where no one lived but himself.

In the fourth year I prospered. I had not only learned the Portuguese language, but had made friends with fellow planters and merchants. In my talk with them, I told them of my voyages to Africa, and the manner of trading with the natives there, and how easy it was to purchase gold and ivory. My friends were so attentive, they decided they wanted me to go to Africa for them and carry on this trading for themselves, for which I would receive an equal share of the goods I bargained for.

I had a plantation of my own to look after; for me

to think of such a voyage was the most preposterous thing that I could have done. But I, who was born my own worst enemy, could not resist my friends' offer. They agreed to take care of my plantation while I was gone.

2
I Arrive on the Desert Island

THE SHIP being fitted out and cargo put aboard, I departed the first of September, 1659, the same day as eight years before I went from my father and mother. Our ship carried six cannons and fourteen men, besides the master of the ship, his servant boy, and myself.

We had good weather all the way up Brazil's coast till we turned east and a violent hurricane took us sailing into unknown parts. For twelve days we could do nothing but let the fury of the winds direct us whatever way it wanted.

Besides the terror of the storm, one of our men died of a tropical fever, and one man and the servant boy washed overboard. About the twelfth day, the weather letting up a little, the shipmaster made an observation as well as he could, and found that we were upon the coast of Guiana, or the north part of Brazil, beyond the Amazon River, towards the Orinoco River. He asked me what course he should take, for the ship was leaky and disabled, to return to the coast of Brazil.

We concluded there was no inhabited country for us to land upon until we came within the circle of the

Caribbean Islands, and therefore decided to make for Barbados, which we might do in about fifteen days' sail.

But our voyage brought us into another storm and drove us so far off our course that were we able to land, we were more likely to be eaten by savages than to ever return to our country.

In this distress, the wind still blowing very hard, one of our men early in the morning cried out, "Land!" We had no sooner run out of the cabin than the ship struck upon the sand, and in a moment, the sea broke over her. We rushed back within our close quarters to shelter us from the waves. We did not know where we were or upon what land it was we were driven, whether an island or mainland, inhabited or not inhabited. We sat looking at each other and expecting death every moment.

The ship having struck upon the sand, and sticking too fast for us to expect her getting off, we were in a dreadful condition. The mate of our ship, however, lay hold of the life boat, and with the help of the rest of the men, they got her slung over the ship's side and, getting all into her, let go and committed ourselves to God's mercy and the wild sea.

We worked at the oars towards the land. But we all felt that when the boat came nearer the shore, she would be dashed in a thousand pieces by the break of the sea. As we made nearer and nearer the shore, the land looked more frightful than the sea.

After we had rowed a few miles, a raging wave,

But our voyage brought us into another storm.

mountain-like, came rolling from behind us. It overset the boat at once, and hardly gave us time to say, "O God!" We were all swallowed up in a moment.

Though I swam very well, I could not get out from under the waves so as to draw breath, till that wave went back, and left me upon the land almost dry, but half dead with the water I swallowed. I got upon my feet and tried to get on towards the land as fast as I could, before another wave should return and take me up again. But I soon found it was impossible to avoid it. I saw the sea come after me as high as a great hill, and as furious as an enemy.

The sea dashed me against a piece of a rock, and with such force that it left me senseless. I held fast to the rock till the wave went back, and then I ran for the shore. I got to the mainland, where, to my great comfort, I clambered up the cliffs to the shore and sat myself down upon the grass, free from danger, and quite out of reach of the water.

I was now landed and safe on shore, and began to look up and thank God that my life was saved. I walked about on the shore, lifting up my hands, reflecting upon all my comrades that were drowned and that there was not a single person left alive but myself. I never saw any sign of them, except three of their hats, one cap, and two unmatched shoes.

I looked out towards the stranded ship, where I could hardly see it, it lay so far off. Lord! how was it possible I could get on shore!

After this I began to look round me to see what

kind of place I was in, and what was next to be done. I was wet, I had no clothes to change into, nor anything to eat or drink. I did not see anything ahead of me but perishing with hunger or being devoured by wild beasts. I had nothing with me but a knife, a tobacco pipe, and a little tobacco in a box. Night was coming upon me. I walked a ways from the shore to see if I could find any fresh water to drink, which I did, to my great joy. Having drunk, I went to a thick, bushy tree and climbed up into it. I put myself into a position so that if I happened to fall asleep, I would not tumble down. I soon fell fast asleep.

When I waked it was broad daylight, the weather clear, and the storm gone. But what surprised me most was the ship had been lifted off in the night from the sand where she had lain, and was driven up almost as far as the rock I first mentioned, where I had been so bruised by being dashed against it. This was within about a mile from the shore where I was and, the ship seeming to stand upright, I wished myself on board, so that I might save some necessary things for my use.

In the afternoon I found the sea very calm and the tide so far out that I could come within a quarter of a mile of the ship. I resolved to get to it, so I pulled off my clothes and swam through the water. When I came to the ship I found a small piece of rope hanging down by which, with great difficulty, I pulled myself up.

My first work was to search and to see what

remaining goods on board were spoiled and what was not. I went to the kitchen and filled my pockets with biscuits. I was very hungry, and ate them as I went about, for I had no time to lose. I also found some rum in the great cabin. Now I needed nothing but a boat to furnish myself with many things which I foresaw would be very necessary to me.

It was no use wishing for a boat, so I built myself a strong raft. I loaded it with boards, seaman's chests filled with provisions (that is, bread, rice, cheese, dried goat meat, grains). While I was doing this, I found the tide began to flow, and I had the disappointed surprise of seeing my coat, shirt, and waistcoat, which I had left on shore upon the sand, swim away. As for my pants, which were only linen, and open-kneed, I swam on board in them and my stockings. However, this got me to rummage for clothes, of which I found enough, but I took no more than I wanted for present use. I had other things which my eye was keener on, for instance tools to work with on shore. I found the carpenter's chest of tools—more valuable to me than a ship full of gold would have been, and got it down to my raft.

My next care was for some ammunition and guns. I secured two small guns and two pistols, with some gunpowder horns and a small bag of gunshot, and two old rusty swords. I found two barrels of dry gunpowder. Now I thought my raft pretty well loaded, and began to think how I should get to shore with this cargo, having neither sail, oar, or rudder. A breeze would have upset the raft.

I had, however, three signs of encouragement: 1. A smooth, calm sea. 2. The tide rising and setting in to shore. 3. What little wind there was blew me towards the land.

And so, having found two or three broken oars belonging to the boat, I set out. I found a strong current of the tide setting into a creek, so I guided my raft as well as I could to keep it in the middle of the stream. But, knowing nothing of the coast, I ran my raft aground upon a sandbank, and all my cargo nearly slipped off. When the tide rose further, after half an hour, the raft floated again, and I at length found myself in the mouth of the little river, with land on both sides. I guided my raft to a little cove and anchored her till the water ebbed away and left my raft and all my cargo safe on shore.

My next piece of work was to view the country, and seek a proper place to live and stow my goods. Where I was I did not know, whether on the continent or on an island; whether inhabited or uninhabited; whether in danger of wild beasts or not. There was a hill not more than a mile from me, which rose up very steep and high, and which seemed to overtop some other hills. I took out one of the small guns and one of the pistols, and a horn of gunpowder, and thus armed I travelled for discovery up to the top of that hill. After I had with great labor and difficulty got to the top, I saw that I was on an island, no land to be seen in any direction across the sea except some rocks that lay a great way off.

I found also that the island was uninhabited, except by wild beasts, of whom, however, I saw none. Yet I saw many birds. On returning from the hilltop I shot a large bird I saw sitting upon a tree near a forest. I believe it was the first gun that had been fired there since the creation of the world. I had no sooner fired than from all parts of the forest there arose innumerable birds of many sorts, making a confused screaming, and crying every one according to his usual note. Not one of them was of any kind that I knew.

I went back to my raft and went to work to bring my cargo on shore, which took me the rest of that day. What to do with myself at night, I did not know. I was afraid to lie down on the ground, thinking that some wild beast might devour me.

However, as well as I could, I barricaded myself round with the chests and boards that I had brought on shore, and made a kind of hut for that night's lodging.

The next day I resolved to make another voyage to the ship and get myself many useful things. I knew that the first storm that blew must necessarily break her all in pieces. My raft appeared unmanageable, so I resolved to swim out as before, when the tide was down.

I got on board the ship as before, and prepared a second raft, and having had experience of the first, I made this more simple. I did not load it as much, but yet I brought back several things useful to me. In the carpenter's storeroom I found two or three bags of nails and spikes, a jack, a dozen or two hatchets and a grindstone. All these I tied together, with several guns and bags of ammunition belonging to the gunner. Besides these things I took all the men's clothes that I could find, and a spare sail, hammock and bedding. With this I loaded my second raft, and brought it all safe on shore.

I went to work to make myself a little tent with the sail and some poles that I had cut for that purpose, and into this tent I brought everything that I knew would spoil, either with rain or sun, and I piled all the empty chests and casks up in a circle round the tent, to fortify it from man or beast. When I had done this, I blocked up the door of the tent with some boards inside, and an empty chest set up on end outside. Spreading one of the beds upon the ground, laying my two pistols just at my head and my gun at length by me, I went to bed for the first time since my arrival, and slept very quietly all night, for I was very weary.

I had the largest store of goods of all kinds now that ever was laid up, I believe, for one man. But I was not satisfied. For while the ship sat upright, I thought I ought to get everything out of her that I could. After I had made five or six voyages, and thought I had nothing more to expect from the ship, I found a great container of bread, and three large casks of rum, a box of sugar, and a barrel of fine flour. After this I went every day on board and brought away what I could get.

After thirteen days on shore, I had been eleven times on board the ship. Preparing the twelfth time to go on board, I found the wind began to rise. However, at low water I went on board, and though I thought I had rummaged the cabin so effectually, as that nothing more could be found, yet I discovered a locker with drawers in it, in one of which I found two or three razors and one pair of large scissors, with some dozen good knives and forks.

I began to think of making another raft, but while I was wrapping up these goods, I found the sky overcast, and the wind began to rise. In a quarter of an hour it blew a fresh gale from the shore. It occurred to me it was folly to make a raft, and that it was my business to be gone before the tide of flood began, otherwise I might not be able to reach the shore at all. And so I let myself down into the water and swam across the channel, which lay between the ship and the sands, and even that with difficulty, partly with the weight of the things I had wrapped up about me, and partly the roughness of the water. The wind rose very quickly. Before it was quite high water, it blew a storm.

But I got home to my little tent, where I lay with all my wealth about me very secure. It blew very hard all that night, and in the morning, when I looked out, behold, no ship was to be seen.

3

I Build My Fortress

MY THOUGHTS were now wholly employed about securing myself against either savages or wild beasts. I had many thoughts of the method how to do this, and what kind of dwelling to make. I wondered whether I should make a cave in the earth, or a tent upon the ground. And, in short, I resolved upon both. I soon found the place I was in was not right for my settlement, particularly because there was no fresh water near it.

I wanted several things for my place. Firstly, health and fresh water. Secondly, shelter from the heat of the sun. Thirdly, security from hungry creatures, whether man or beast. Fourthly, a view to the sea, so that if any ship came in sight, I might not lose a chance for my rescue.

I found a little plain on the side of a hill. The rocky hillside facing the plain was very steep. This was good, because nothing then could come down upon me from the top. On the side of this rock there was a hollow place worn a little way like the entrance or door of a cave, but there was not really any cave or way into the rock at all.

On the flat of the green just before this hollow

place, I pitched my tent. This plain was not more than a hundred yards wide, and about twice as long, and lay like a lawn before my door, and at the end of it dropped every which way down into the low grounds by the seaside. It was on the north-northwest side of the hill, so that I was sheltered from the heat every day.

Before I set up my tent I drew a half circle before the hollow place. In this half circle I drove two rows of strong stakes, the longer end being out of the ground about five foot and a half, and sharpened on the top. Then I took the pieces of cable I had cut from the ship, and laid them in rows one upon another, within the circle between these two rows of stakes. This fence was so strong that neither man nor beast could get into it or over it.

The entrance into this place I made to be not by a door but by a short ladder to go over the top. The ladder, when I was in, I lifted over after me. In this way I was completely fenced in, and fortified from all the world, and so slept well in the night.

Into this fence or fortress I carried, with much labor, all my riches, all my provisions, ammunition and goods. I made a large doubled tent to protect me from the rains that in one part of the year are very violent there. Now I lay no more in the bed which I had brought on the shore, but in a hammock, which was indeed a very good one.

When I had brought into the tent all my goods, I began to work my way into the rock. I made a cave just behind my tent, which then served me like a cellar to my house.

In the many days which this took me, I went out at least once every day with my gun, as much to amuse myself as to see if I could kill anything fit for food. The first time I went out, I discovered there were goats on the island. But they were so shy, so swift, that it was the most difficult thing in the world to get near them. However, after I had found their haunts, I laid in wait for them. I observed, if they saw me in the valleys, they would run away. But if they were feeding in the valleys, and I was upon the rocks, they took no notice of me. Their eyes were so directed downward, that they did not see objects that were above them. I then always climbed the rocks first, to get above them, and then was able to shoot them for my food somewhat easily.

It was, by my account, the thirtieth of September when I first set foot upon this horrid island. After I had been there about ten or twelve days, it came into my thoughts that I should lose my reckoning of time and should even be unable to tell the Sabbath days from the working days. To prevent this forgetfulness, I cut with my knife upon a large post, on the shore where I landed: "I CAME ON SHORE THE 30TH OF SEPTEMBER 1659." Upon the sides of this square post I cut every day a notch with my knife, and every seventh notch was twice as long as the rest. Every first day of the month was twice as long as that long one. In this way I kept my calendar.

I discovered there were goats on the island.

Among the many things I brought off the ship in the several voyages I made to it, I got several useful things I have not mentioned: pens, ink and paper, compasses, perspectives, charts and books of navigation. Also I found three very good Bibles; some Portuguese books also. I must not forget that we had on the ship a dog and two cats, of whose story I may say something. I carried both the cats with me. As for the dog, he jumped out of the ship by himself, and swam on shore to me the day after I went on shore with my first cargo. He was a trusty servant to me for many years.

While my ink lasted, I kept things very exact. After it was gone, I could not find any way to make more.

My lack of enough tools made every job I did difficult, and it was near a whole year before I had entirely finished the little wall in front of my settlement. I have already described my habitation, which was a tent under the side of a rock, surrounded with a strong wall of posts and cables. After a year and a half, I raised rafters from the wall to the rock, and thatched them with boughs of trees and such things as I could get to keep out the rain.

I also set to enlarge my cave farther into the hillside. It was composed of loose sandy rock, which gave in easily to the work I put in at it. And so, when I found I was pretty safe from beasts of prey, I worked sideways to the right hand into the rock; and then turning to the right again, worked quite out, and made a door to come out on the outside of my wall.

This gave me not only entry and retreat but gave me room to store my goods.

Now I began to make such necessary things as I found I most wanted, particularly a chair and a table. Without these I was not able to enjoy the few comforts I had in the world. I could not write or eat with so much pleasure without a table.

So I went to work. Here I must say that every man may in time be master of every mechanical art. I had never handled a tool in my life, and yet in time, by labor, persistence, and contrivance, I found at last that whatever I needed, I could have made it, especially if I had tools. However, I made many things even without tools, and some with no tools but an adze[1] and hatchet. For example, if I wanted a board, I had no other way than to cut down a tree, set it on an edge before me, and hew it flat on either side with my axe, till I had made it as thin as a plank, and then smooth it with my adze.

And now it was when I began to keep a journal of every day's activity. At first I was in too much of a hurry in my work and in my mind. But having settled my household, I wrote as long as my ink lasted.

(I shall omit from this journal most of those details which I have already related.)

---

[1]*adze*] a cutting tool used for shaping wood.

4
The Journal

October 31. In the morning I went out into the island with my gun to look for some food. I killed a goat, and her kid followed me home.

November 3. I went out with my gun and killed two fowls like ducks, which were very good food. In the afternoon I went to work to make a table.

November 4. This morning I began to order my times of work, of going out with my gun, time of sleep, and time of amusement. Every morning I walked out with my gun for two or three hours, if it did not rain, and worked till about eleven o'clock. Then I ate what I had, and from twelve to two I lay down to sleep, the weather being too hot to be outside. Then in the evening I set to work again.

November 5. This day I went out with my gun and my dog, and killed a wild cat. Every creature I killed, I took off the skins and preserved them. Coming back by the seashore, I was surprised, and almost frightened, by two or three seals, which, while I was gazing at them, not knowing what they were, got into the sea and escaped.

November 6. After my morning walk, I went to work on making my table again, and finished it, though not to my liking.

November 7. Now it began to be fair weather. The 7th, 8th, 9th, 10th, and part of the 12th (for the 11th was a Sunday) I took to make a chair, and with much effort brought it to a passable shape, but not good enough to please me, and even in the making I pulled it to pieces several times. NOTE: I soon gave up taking my Sundays off. Having failed to make my mark for them on my calendar post, I forgot which day was which.

November 13. This day it rained, which refreshed me very much, and cooled the earth, but it came with terrible thunder and lightning, which frightened me dreadfully, for fear of my gunpowder. As soon as it was over, I resolved to separate my stock of gunpowder into as many little packets as possible, that it might not be in danger of exploding.

November 14, 15, 16. These three days I spent in making little square boxes, which might hold about a pound or two pounds, at most, of gunpowder. And so, putting the powder in, I stowed it in places as safe and far from one another as possible.

* * *

December 17. From this day to the 20th, I placed shelves and knocked nails into the posts to hang everything up that could be hung up. And now I began to have some order inside my cave.

December 20. Now I carried everything into the cave, and began to furnish my house, and set up some pieces of boards like a dresser, to arrange my food supplies. But boards began to be very scarce with me. Also I made me another table.

December 24. Much rain all night and all day; no stirring out.

December 25. Rain all day.

December 26. No rain, and the earth much cooler than before, and pleasanter.

December 27. Killed a young goat, and lamed another, so that I caught it, and led it home on a string. When I had it home, I bound and splintered up its leg, which was broken. I took such care of it that it lived, and the leg grew well, and as strong as ever. But by nursing it so long it grew tame, and fed upon the little green at my door, and would not go away. This was the first time that I thought of breeding some tame goats, so that I might have food when my gunpowder and gunshot was all gone.

December 28, 29, 30. Terrible heat and no breeze. There was no going out, except in the evening for food. This time I spent putting all my things in order.

January 1. Very hot still, but I went out early and late with my gun, and lay quiet during the day. This evening going farther into the valleys, which lay towards the center of the island, I found there were plenty of goats, though very shy and hard to get at.

From the 3rd of January to the 14th of April, I was working, finishing and perfecting the wall outside my habitation.

During this time, I made my rounds in the woods for food every day when the rain let me, and made many discoveries in these walks of something or other for my own good. Particularly, I found a kind of wild pigeon, which had very good meat.

In the managing of my household affairs, I found myself in need of many things, which I thought at first it was impossible for me to make, as indeed for some of them it was. I was in great need for candles. As soon as it was dark, which was generally by seven o'clock, I had to go to bed. The only solution I had was that, when I would kill a goat, I saved the fat, and with a little dish I made of clay, which I baked in the sun, to which I added a wick of rope fiber, I made me a lamp. This gave me light, though not a clear, steady light like a candle.

In the middle of all my projects it happened that, rummaging through my things, I found a little bag, which had been filled with grain for birds. I saw nothing in the bag now but husks and dust. Wanting the bag for some other use, I shook the husks of grain out of it to one side of my fort.

It was a little before the great rains that I threw this stuff away, taking no notice of anything, and not so much as remembering that I had thrown anything there. About a month after, I saw some few stalks of something green shooting out of the ground, which I imagined might be some plant I had not seen. But I was surprised when after a little longer time I saw about ten or twelve ears of green barley, of the same kind as our English barley.

I carefully saved the ears of this grain, you may be sure. Storing up every seed, I resolved to plant them all again, hoping in time to have enough to supply myself with bread. It was not until the fourth year that I could let myself eat the smallest part of this crop.

But to return to my journal.

June 16. Going down to the seaside, I found a large turtle. This was the first I had seen, which it seems was only my bad luck, not any fault of the place or lack of them. Had I happened to be on the other side of the island, I might have had hundreds of them every day.

June 17. This day I spent in cooking the turtle. I found in her sixty eggs. This turtle was to me the best and most pleasant meat that I ever tasted in my life, having eaten nothing but goats and birds since I had landed on this horrid place.

June 21. Very ill, frightened almost to death with my fears of my sad condition, to be sick and have no help. Prayed to God for the first time since my first ship adventure, but hardly knew what I said, my thoughts being all confused.

From the 4th of July to the 14th I was mostly busy in walking about with my gun in my hand, a little at a time, as I was a man that was gathering up his strength after a fit of sickness.

I had been now on this miserable island more than ten months. All possibility of rescue seemed gone. I firmly believed that no human shape had ever set foot upon that place. Having now made my home safe, I had a great desire to make a fuller discovery of the island and to see what other things I could find.

It was the 15th of July when I began to take a closer look at the island. I went up the creek first, where I had brought my rafts from the wrecked ship on shore.

I found, after I went about two miles up, that the tide did not flow any higher, and that it was no more than a brook of running water, and very fresh and good. But this was the dry season, and there was hardly any water in some parts of it.

On the bank of this brook, I found many pleasant meadows.

The next day, the 16th, I went up the same way again, and after going somewhat farther than I had gone the day before, I found the brook and the meadows began to disappear, and the country became more woody than before. In this part I found different fruits, and particularly I found melons upon the ground in great abundance, and grapes upon the trees, and the clusters of grapes were just now in their prime, very ripe and rich. I found an excellent use for these grapes, and that was to dry them in the sun and keep them as raisins, which I thought would be, as indeed they were, as wholesome and good to eat when no grapes might be had.

I spent all that evening there. In the night I got up into a tree, where I slept well. The next morning I proceeded on my discovery, travelling near four miles, keeping due north, with a ridge of hills on the south and north side of me. I came to a clearing where the country seemed to descend to the west, and a little spring of fresh water, which issued out of the side of the hill by me, ran due east. The country appeared to me so fresh, so green, so flourishing, that it looked like a planted garden.

I went down a little on the side of that beautiful valley, looking it over with a secret kind of pleasure, to think that this country was all my own, that I was king and lord of all this country. I saw here many cocoa trees, orange and lemon and citron trees. But all of them were wild and very few were bearing any fruit, at least not then. However, the limes that I gathered were not only pleasant to eat but very wholesome. I mixed their juice afterwards with water, which made it very wholesome and very cool and refreshing.

When I came home from this journey, I thought with great pleasure about the fruitfulness of that valley and the pleasantness of the place, the security from storms on that side of the water and the forest.

I spent much of my time there for the whole remaining part of the month of July. I built myself a little kind of a shelter and surrounded it at a distance with a strong fence, being a double hedge as high as I could reach. And here I lay very secure, sometimes two or three nights in a row. I fancied now I had my country house and my seacoast house. And this work took me up to the beginning of August.

I had recently finished my fence and began to enjoy the efforts of my work. The 3rd of August I found the grapes I had hung up were perfectly dried, and were excellent raisins. No sooner had I taken them down and carried most of them to my cave than it began to rain and from here on, which was the 14th of August, it rained more or less every day, till the middle of October; and sometimes so violently that I could not stir out of my cave for several days.

From the 14th of August to the 26th, there was such steady rain that I could not stir, and I was now very careful not to get too wet. In this confinement I began to be short of food, but venturing out twice, I one day killed a goat. And the last day, which was the 26th, I found a very large turtle, which was a treat to me. I ate a bunch of raisins for my breakfast; a piece of broiled goat or turtle meat for my lunch; and two or three of the turtle's eggs for my supper.

September 30. I was now come to the unhappy anniversary of my landing. I counted up the notches on my calendar post, and found I had been on shore three hundred and sixty-five days. I kept this date as a solemn fast day, setting it apart to religious exercise, confessing my sins to God, and praying to Him to have mercy upon me. Having not tasted the least bit of food for twelve hours, I then ate a biscuit and a bunch of grapes, and went to bed.

A little after this my ink began to fail me, and so I forced myself to use it less, and to write down only the most remarkable events of my life, without continuing a daily journal.

I mentioned before that I wanted to see the whole island, and that I had travelled up the brook, and so on to where I built my second shelter. I now resolved to travel quite across to the seashore on that side. When I had passed the valley where my shelter stood, I came to within view of the sea to the west. It was a very clear day, and I saw land. I knew it must be part of South America. Perhaps it was inhabited by savages, and if I had landed there, I would have been in a worse condition than I was now. For they are cannibals and fail not to murder and devour all the human bodies that fall into their hands.

I found this side of the island, where I now was, much pleasanter than mine, the open meadows sweet, adorned with flowers and grass, and full of fine woods. I saw many parrots. After some painstaking, I did catch a young parrot, and I brought it home. It was, however, some years before I could make him speak.

I travelled along the shore of the sea, towards the east, about twelve miles; and then setting up a great pole upon the shore for a marker, I decided I would go home again; and that the next journey I took should be on the other side of the island, east from my dwelling, and so round till I came to the post again.

I was very impatient to be at home, from where I had been gone more than a month. I cannot express what a satisfaction it was to me to come into my old home and lie down in my hammock. I relaxed here for a week, to rest myself after my long journey. During that week, most of the time was taken up with making a cage for my parrot.

When the rainy season came again, I kept the 30th of September in the same manner as before. This date was the anniversary of my landing on the island, and I had now been there two years.

5

I Am Very Seldom Idle

THUS I began my third year. It may be observed that I was very seldom idle. I had regularly divided my time, going out every day for food, which generally took me three hours every morning. Then I was organizing, preserving and cooking what I had killed or caught for my supply. These duties took up a great part of the day. My labors took many hours, as I lacked tools, help and skill. For example, it took forty-two days for me to make a long shelf for my cave; whereas two carpenters with their tools would have cut six of them out of the same tree in half a day.

My case was this: it was a large tree which I had to cut down, because my board was to be a wide one. This tree I was three days cutting down, and two more cutting off the boughs, and reducing it to a log. With hacking and shaving, I reduced both sides of it into chips, till it began to be light enough to move. Then I turned it and made one side of it smooth and flat; then turning that side downward, cut the other side, till I made the plank about three inches thick and smooth on both sides.

I was now in the months of November and December, expecting my crop of barley and rice which I had planted earlier. The ground I had manured and dug up for them was not large, but I found I was in danger of losing it all to enemies of several kinds. At first, it was the goats and the rabbits. I got my plot totally well fenced in in about three weeks' time. Having shot some of the raiding creatures in the daytime, I set my dog to guard it in the night, tying him up to a stake at the gate, where he would stand and bark all night long. In a little time the enemies gave up the place, and the grain grew very strong and well, and began to ripen.

But as the beasts ruined me before, while my grain was growing, the birds were as likely to ruin me now, when it was ripening. I foresaw that in a few days they would devour all my hopes. I killed three of the birds and hanged them to frighten away the others, and this was very effective.

At the latter end of December, I reaped my crop. I had a hard job, as I did not have a sickle to cut it down, and all I could do was to make one as well as I could out of one of the swords I had saved from the ship.

I foresaw that in time it would please God to supply me with bread. And yet here I was perplexed again, for I neither knew how to grind or make meal of my grain, or indeed how to clean it and separate it. Even if I had had meal, I did not know how to make bread of it. And even if I had known how to make it, I did not know how I would be able to bake it. I preserved this crop all for seed for the next season, and in the meantime tried to figure out a way to make bread for myself.

At the latter end of December, I reaped my crop.

But first I had to prepare more land, for I had now seed enough to plant more than an acre. I planted my seed in two large flat pieces as near my house as I could find them, and fenced them in with a good hedge. This work took me nearly three months, because a large part of that time was during the wet season, when I could not go out.

When I stayed inside and while I was at work on something, I amused myself with talking to my parrot and teaching him to speak. I quickly taught him to know his own name and at last to speak it out loud, "Poll," which was the first word I ever heard spoken on the island by any mouth but my own.

I had long been studying how to make myself some clay vessels, which indeed I wanted very much, but did not know how to do so. It would make the reader pity me, or rather laugh at me, to tell how many awkward ways I took to make this pasty clay. What odd, misshapen, ugly things I made! How many of them fell in, and how many fell apart, the clay not being stiff enough to bear its own weight. How many of the vessels cracked by the too hot sun. After having worked so hard to find the clay, to dig it, to bring it home and work it, I could not make more than two large clay ugly things, I cannot call them jars, in about two months' labor.

Though I botched so much in my design for large pots, yet I made several smaller things with better success; such as little round pots, flat dishes, pitchers and anything my hand turned to, and the heat of the sun baked them hard.

But all this would not satisfy my need, which was to get a clay pot to hold a liquid and bear the fire, which none of these could do. It happened after some time, making a pretty large fire for cooking my meat, when I went to put it out after I had done with it, I found a broken piece of one of my clay vessels in the fire, burnt hard as a stone, and red as a tile. I was surprised to see it, and said to myself that certainly they might be made to burn whole, if they would burn broken.

This set me to studying how to arrange my fire, so as to make it burn some pots. I placed several large pots in a pile one upon another and placed my firewood all around it with a great heap of embers under them; I added to the fire with fresh fuel round the outside and on top, till I saw the pots in the inside red hot quite through, and observed that they did not crack at all. When I saw them clear red, I let them stand in that heat about five or six hours, till I found one of them, though it did not crack, did run, for the sand which was mixed with the clay melted, and would have run into glass if I had gone on. So I slacked my fire, and found in the morning I had five very good, I will not say handsome, pots. One of them, indeed, was perfectly glazed with the running of the sand.

No joy was ever equal to mine, when I found I had made a clay pot that would bear the fire. I had hardly patience to wait till they were cold, before I set one upon the fire again, with some water in it, to boil me some meat, which it did well. With a piece of goat I made some very good broth.

My next concern was to get a mortar to grind some grain in it. I found a great block of hard wood, and I rounded it and formed it to make a hollow place in it. To separate the bran from the husk of the grain I made a sieve from some muslin neckerchiefs. I made some very wide clay vessels and used these as ovens for my bread, which I had learned to make.

It need not be wondered at, if all these things took me the most part of the third year of my life here.

I began thinking whether it was not possible to make myself a canoe, such as the natives of these climates make, even without tools, from the trunk of a large tree.

I pleased myself with the plan for one, without figuring out whether I would ever be able to complete it and get the boat from its place to the water. "Let's first make it," I told myself. "I'll find some way or other to get it out of here, once it's done."

This was a ridiculous method. But the eagerness of my imagination won out, and to work I went. I chopped down a cedar tree. It took me twenty days of hacking and chipping at its base to chop it down. I was two weeks more getting the branches and limbs off. After this it cost me a month to shape it and get it something like the bottom of a boat, that it might swim upright as it ought to do. It cost me near three months more to clear the inside, and work it out so as to make an exact boat of it. This I did without fire, with mere mallet and chisel. I made it a very hand-some canoe, big enough to have carried twenty-six men, or big enough to have carried me and all my cargo.

I was extremely delighted with it. The boat was really much bigger than I ever saw a canoe that was made of one tree. There remained nothing but to get it into the water. Had I gotten it into the water, I have no doubt but I should have begun the craziest voyage ever undertaken.

But all my attempts to get it into the water failed me. The boat lay about one hundred yards from the water.

In the middle of this work I finished my fourth year in this place, and kept my anniversary with the same devotion as before.

6

I Travel Around the Island

MY CLOTHES began to decay. It was a very great help to me that I had among all the men's clothes of the ship almost three dozen shirts. There were also several thick seamen's coats, but they were too hot to wear. Though it is true that the weather was so violently hot that there was no need of clothes, yet I could not go quite naked. No, even had I wanted to, which I did not, I could not bear the heat of the sun so well when quite naked, as with some clothes on. With my shirt on, the air itself made some motion, and under that shirt I was twice as cool than without it. I could not bring myself to go out in the heat of the sun without a cap or a hat.

I have mentioned that I saved the skins of all the creatures that I killed, and I hung them up and stretched them out with sticks in the sun, by which means some of them were so dry and hard that they were fit for little, but others were very useful. The first thing I made of these was a cap for my head, with the fur on the outside, to put off the rain. I made this so well, that after this I made a suit of clothes out of these skins. That is to say, a waistcoat, and pants open at the knees, and both loose, for they were more for keeping me cool than to keep me warm. I must not fail to say that they were poorly made; for if I was a bad carpenter, I was a worse tailor. However, they were such as I did very well by them; and when I was out, if it happened to rain, the fur of my waistcoat and cap kept me very dry.

After this I spent a great deal of time and pains to make an umbrella. The main difficulty I found was to make it let down. I could make it spread, but if it did not let down too and draw in, it was not portable for me any way but just over my head, which would not do. However, at last, I made one that worked, and covered it with skins.

I cannot say that after this, for five years, any extraordinary thing happened to me, but I lived on in the same way, in the same place. The chief thing I was busy with, besides my yearly labor of planting my barley and rice and drying my raisins and my daily labor of going out with my gun, was to make me a canoe, which at last I finished. As for the first canoe, which was so big that I was never able to bring it to the water, I had to let it lie where it was. However, though my little canoe was finished, it was not big enough to do what I had wanted my boat to do, which was to venture from my island to the mainland forty miles off across the sea. But as I had a boat, my next plan was to make a tour around the island.

For this, I fitted up a little mast to my boat, and made a sail to it out of some of the pieces of the ship's sail. I found the boat would sail very well. Then

I made little boxes at either end of my boat, to put provisions, necessities, and ammunition, etc., into, to be kept dry.

I fixed my umbrella also in a slot at the stern, like a mast, to stand over my head, and keep the heat of the sun off of me like an awning. In this way I every now and then took a little voyage upon the sea, but never went far out, nor far from the little creek. But at last being eager to see all the way around my little kingdom, I resolved upon my tour and so packed for the voyage, putting in two dozen of my cakes of barley bread, a clay pot full of cooked rice, a little bottle of rum, half a goat, and gunpowder and gunshot for killing more goats, and two large coats to use as blankets in the night.

It was the 6th of November, in the sixth year of my kingship, that I set out on this voyage, and I found it much longer than I expected. For though the island was not very large, yet when I came to the east side of it, I found a great ledge of rocks lie out a few miles into the sea, some above water, some under it, so that I had to go a great way out to sea to get around the point.

A current carried my boat along with it with such strength that all I could do could not prevent my being driven into the vast ocean. I was taken a frightful distance from the island, and had the least cloud or hazy weather come between me and it, I should have been lost, for I had no compass on board, and should never have known how to have steered towards the island, if I had lost sight of it.

When I finally got back to shore, I fell on my knees and gave God thanks for my deliverance, resolving to give up all thoughts of my escape from the island by my boat.

After I slept near the beach that night, I had no idea how I would get home with my boat. I had been in so much danger that I would not think of going back the way I had come there. What might be on the other side, I did not know, and did not desire to take any more chances. So I coasted along the shore about three miles, and came to a bay, which narrowed until it became a brook, where I found a safe harbor for my boat.

I soon found I had barely passed by the place where I had been when I travelled on foot to the shore. So, taking nothing out of my boat but my gun and my umbrella, I began my march to my country shelter, where I found everything as I had left it.

I got over the fence and laid me down in the shade to rest my limbs, for I was very weary, and fell asleep. But think of what a surprise I felt, when I was waked out of my sleep by a voice calling me by my name several times, "Robin, Robin, Robin Crusoe, poor Robin Crusoe! Where are you, Robin Crusoe? Where are you? Where have you been?"

I was so dead asleep at first, being tired with paddling the first part of the day, that I did not wake completely. But dozing between sleeping and waking, I thought I dreamed that somebody spoke to me. But

as the voice continued to repeat "Robin Crusoe,
Robin Crusoe," at last I began to wake fully, and was
at first dreadfully frightened and started up in confusion. But no sooner were my eyes open, but I saw
my Poll sitting on the top of the hedge; and immediately I knew that it was he that spoke to me. It was
just in such language I had used to talk to him, and
teach him. He had learned it so perfectly that he
would sit upon my finger and lay his bill close to my
face, and cry, "Poor Robin Crusoe! Where are you?
Where have you been? How did you come here?"

However, even though I knew it was the parrot, and
that indeed it could be nobody else, it was a while
before I could calm down. But when I got over it, I
called out, "Poll," and he came to me, and sat upon
my thumb, and continued talking to me, "Poor Robin
Crusoe! How did you come here? Where have you
been?" It was just as if he had been overjoyed to see
me again. And so I carried him home along with me.

For the next year I lived a very calm life. I arrived at
an unexpected skill in my pottery. I made things
round and well-shaped which before were filthy things
indeed to look at. But I think I was never more vain of
my own work than for being able to make a tobacco
pipe. And though it was a very ugly, clumsy thing
when it was done, it was firm, and would draw the
smoke, and I was very comforted with it.

Being now in the eleventh year of my residence,
and my ammunition growing low, I set myself to
study some art to trap and snare the goats, to see

whether I could catch some of them alive. I particularly wanted a pregnant she-goat. I made pits and caught three kids, and taking them one by one, I tied them with strings together and brought them all home.

It was a while before they would feed, but by throwing them some sweet grain, it tempted them and they began to be tame. And now I found if I expected to supply myself with goat-meat when I had no gunpowder or gunshot left, breeding some up tame was my only way.

But then it occurred to me that I needed to have some enclosed ground, well-fenced, to keep them penned in. This was a great chore for one pair of hands, yet as I saw the need for doing it, I did it. It took me about three months to hedge in my first piece of ground. In about a year and a half I had a flock of about twelve goats, kids and all. In two years more I had forty-three, besides several that I ate. Now I had not only goat meat to eat when I liked, but milk too. I set up my dairy and had sometimes a gallon or two of milk a day.

I was finally impatient to have the use of my boat again, though not wanting to have any more dangerous adventures. At length I resolved to travel to the other side of the island by land, following the edge of the shore. Had anyone in England to meet such a man as I looked, it must either have frightened them or caused a great deal of laughter. Imagine how I appeared:

I had a large, high shapeless cap, made of a goat's skin, with a flap hanging down behind, as well to keep the sun from me as to ward off the rain from running down my neck. I had a jacket of goatskin that came down to about the middle of my thighs, and a pair of open-kneed pants of the same material. I did not have any shoes or socks, but I had made myself a pair of somethings, I hardly know what to call them, to flap over my legs, and lace on either side.

I had a broad belt of goatskin, and loops, where I hung a little saw and a hatchet. I had another belt, over my shoulder, and at the end of it, under my left arm, hung two pouches. In one of the pouches was my gunpowder, and in the other my gunshot. At my back I carried a basket, on my shoulder my gun, and over my head a large, clumsy, ugly goatskin umbrella. My beard I once allowed to grow till it was about a foot long. But as I had both scissors and razors, I cut it pretty short, except for my moustache, which I trimmed to look the way a Turk's would.

7

I Find the Print of a Man's Naked Foot

IT HAPPENED one day about noon, going towards my boat on the other side of the island. I was very surprised with the print of a man's naked foot on the shore, which was very plain to be seen in the sand. I stood like one thunderstruck, or as if I had seen a ghost. I listened, I looked round me, I could hear nothing, nor see anything. I went up to a rising ground to look farther. I went up the shore and down the shore, but I could see no more prints than that one. I went to it again to see if there were any more, and to check if it might not be my imagination. But there it was, the exact print of a foot, toes, heel and every part of a foot. How it came to be there I did not know, nor could in the least imagine. But after many confusing thoughts, I went home, terrified, looking behind me every two or three steps, mistaking every bush and tree, and imagining every stump at a distance to be a man.

When I arrived at my castle, I fled into it like one pursued. There had never been a more frightened rabbit or fox fleeing to cover, than I had been returning to my fort.

I did not sleep at all that night. After convincing

I was very surprised with the print of a man's naked foot
on the shore.

myself that the print had not been left by the Devil, I concluded that then it must be an even more dangerous creature, that is, some of the savages of the mainland, who had wandered out to sea in their canoes. Then terrible thoughts racked my imagination about their having found my boat, and that there were people here. If so, they would certainly come again in larger numbers and devour me.

For three days and nights I stayed within my cave, and then it came into my head that all these thoughts about the footprint might have been the result of an illusion, that this foot might be the print of my own foot, when I came on shore from my boat. I began to gain courage and to peep outside again. After I resumed my former routine, and began venturing to my goats, I decided to return to the shore and see this print of a foot, and measure it against my own, that I might know if it was indeed my foot. But when I came to the place, first it appeared obvious to me that when I laid up my boat, I could not possibly have been on shore anywhere near there. Secondly, when I came to measure the mark with my own foot, I found my foot much smaller. Both these things filled my head with new fancies, and gave me the terrors again. I went home again, filled with the belief that some man or men had been on shore there. I imagined that the island was inhabited, and I might be surprised before I was aware. What I should do for my safety, I did not know.

I concluded that this island, which was so pleasant,

fruitful and not so very far from the mainland, was not so entirely desolate as I had imagined. I had lived here fifteen years now, and had not met with the least shadow or figure of any people yet. If at any time the savages should be driven here, it was probable they went away again as soon as ever they could.

I had nothing to do but to think of some safe retreat, in case I should see any savages land upon the spot. I made a second wall of trees around my first wall, and in two years had a thick grove. In five or six years' time I had an impassable forest in front of my dwelling. No man of any kind would ever imagine there was anything beyond it. As for the way I got in and out, I now had two ladders; one to a part of the rock which was low and had a ledge, where I placed another ladder.

While all this was going on, I was not careless of my other affairs; for I had great concern for my little herd of goats. I decided to separate my goats into two remote, hidden spots, that the savages might not find them. One spot I found was a little piece of open ground in the middle of the thick woods.

All this effort and labor came about because of my fears on account of the man's footprint, and for the next two years I lived with less comfort than before. After I had found the one hidden pen for half of my goats, I went around the whole island searching for another private place. When wandering more to the west point of the island than I had ever done yet, and looking out to sea, I thought I saw a boat upon the sea, at a great distance. I had found a spyglass in one of the seaman's chests from the ship; but I did not have it with me.

When I came down the hill to the shore, I was horrified and amazed to see the shore covered with skulls, hands, feet and other bones of human bodies. I observed a place where there had been a fire, and a circle dug in the earth, where I supposed the savages had sat down to their terrible feastings upon the bodies of their fellow creatures.

I turned and ran up the hill again, and then walked home to my castle. I felt that as I had been here now almost eighteen years, I might be here eighteen more if I stayed as hidden as I had been. Within a few days, I began to live in the same calm way as before. It was only with this difference, that I used more caution, and kept my eyes more alert than I did before. I was more cautious about firing my gun, to prevent any of them, did they happen to be on the island, from hearing it. It was therefore fortunate that I had provided myself with a herd of tame goats, so that I did not have to hunt any more for them through the woods or shoot at them. For two years after this, I believe I never fired my gun off once, though I never went out without it. What was more, as I had saved three pistols out of the ship, I always carried them out with me, or at least two of them, sticking them in my goatskin belt. I was now a most imposing looking fellow when I went out, if you add to the earlier description of myself the two pistols and a large sword, hanging at my side by the belt.

I seldom went out from my cave other than to milk my she-goats and manage my little flock in the woods. I had the care of my safety more now upon my hands than that of my food. I did not want to drive a nail or chop a piece of wood now, for fear the noise I should make should be heard. Above all, I was worried about making a fire, as the smoke, which is visible at a great distance in the day, should betray me. And for this reason I moved that part of my business which required fire, such as burning pots, into a natural cave in the earth, which was deep, and where, I dare say, no savage, had he been at the mouth of it, would be so courageous as to go in.

I was now in my twenty-third year of living on this island and was so used to the place and to the way of living that could I have been certain that no savages would come, I could have been content to spend the rest of my life here. I had also managed some amusements, which made the time pass more pleasantly than it did before. I had taught my parrot, Poll, to speak. He did it so well, that it was very pleasant to me. My dog was a very pleasant and loving companion to me for no less than sixteen years of my time, and then died of mere old age. Besides these, I always kept two or three household kids about me, which I taught to feed out of my hand. And I had two more parrots, which talked pretty well, and would all call "Robin Crusoe," but none like my first. I had also several tame sea birds, which I caught along the shore, and clipped their wings. These birds now lived among the wall of trees in front of my home and bred there.

8
I Meet Friday

I WAS SURPRISED one morning to see at least five
canoes all on shore together on my side of the
island. The people who had come in on them all had
landed and were out of my sight. I retreated to my fort
and climbed the rock above my cave with my ladders
and spied the site with my glass. There were about
thirty savages, and they had a fire started and were
cooking meat. They were all dancing round the fire.

While I was watching them, I saw two miserable
men dragged from the boats, where, it seemed, they
had been kept, and were now brought out for killing.
One of the two immediately fell, being knocked down,
I suppose, with a club, and while two or three of the
savages killed him, the other victim was left standing
by himself till they should be ready for him. In that
very moment, the remaining victim saw his chance
and dashed away and ran across the sands in my
direction.

I saw a group run after him. There was between
them and my castle the creek which I mentioned
often at the first part of my story, when I landed my
cargoes out of the ship. This creek I saw he must
swim over, or the poor man would be captured there.

The escaping savage made nothing of the obstacle, but plunged into the creek, swam through it in about thirty strokes, landed and ran on with great strength and swiftness. When the three savages in pursuit came to the creek, two swam after, but the third did not and returned to the others, which, as it happened, was very lucky for him.

I saw that it was now my time to get a friend or servant, and that I was called by God to save this poor escaping creature's life. I immediately ran down the ladders, fetched my two guns, went back up over the ladders, and down hill towards the sea. I hurried to put myself in between the pursuers and the pursued, helloing aloud to the one that was fleeing, who, looking back, was at first perhaps as frightened of me as of them. But I beckoned with my hand to him to come back, and in the meantime I slowly went towards the two that followed. Then, rushing at once upon the first of them, I knocked him down with the butt of my gun. I did not want to fire my gun, because I did not want the others to hear. Having knocked this fellow down, his comrade stopped, as if he was frightened. I now went towards him. But as I came nearer, I saw he had a bow and arrow, and was getting it ready to shoot me. So I had to shoot at him first; which I did, and I killed him at the first shot.

The poor savage who had escaped, though he saw both his enemies fallen, yet was so frightened by the fire and noise of my gun, that he stood still and neither came forward or went away. I helloed again to him, and made signs to come forward, which he understood and came a little way, then stopped again, and then a little farther, and stopped again. And I could see that he stood trembling, as if he had been taken prisoner by me and was about to be killed, as his two enemies were. I beckoned him again to come to me, and gave him all the signs of encouragement I could think of. He came nearer and nearer, kneeling down every ten or twelve steps in thanks for my saving his life.

I smiled at him and looked pleasantly and beckoned him to come still closer. Finally, he came close to me, and then he kneeled down again, kissed the ground, and laid his head upon the ground, and taking me by the foot, set my foot upon his head. I made him get up and tried to make him more at ease. But there was more work to do yet, as I saw the savage whom I knocked down was not killed, but stunned with the blow, and began to come to. So I pointed to him, and showed him the savage, that he was not dead. Upon this he spoke some words to me, and though I could not understand them, yet I thought they were pleasant to hear, for they were the first sound of a man's voice that I had heard, not counting my own, for more than twenty-five years. The savage who was knocked down recovered himself so well as to sit up on the ground. When I pointed my gun at the man as if I would shoot him, my savage made a motion to me to lend him my sword, so I did. He no sooner had it, but he ran to his enemy and at one blow cut off his head. When he had done this, he came laughing to me in triumph and brought me the sword again, and with many gestures I did not understand, laid it down in front of me.

He then buried his two enemies, and then I called him to follow me, and I brought him to my cave, on the farther side of the island. Here I gave him bread and a bunch of raisins to eat, and a drink of water. Having fed him, I made signs for him to go lie down and sleep, pointing to a place where I had put down a great load of straw, and a blanket upon it. So the poor creature lay down and went to sleep.

He was a handsome fellow, with straight, strong limbs, tall, and well-shaped, and about twenty-six years old. He had a manly face, and a sweet and soft look, especially when he smiled. His hair was long and black, and his skin was dark. His face was round and plump; his nose was small, his lips were thin, and his fine teeth were white as ivory.

After he had napped for half an hour, he woke up and came out of the cave to me, where I had been milking the goats, who had their pen nearby. When he saw me he came running, then lay himself down again on the ground, with all the possible signs of a humble, thankful feeling, to let me know he would serve me as long as he lived. In a little while, I began to speak to him and teach him to speak to me. First, I made him know his name should be Friday, which was the day I saved his life. I likewise taught him to say "Master," and then let him know that was to be my name. I likewise taught him to say "yes" and "no" and to know their meaning.

I stayed there with him all that night, but as soon as it was day, I asked him to come with me, and led him up to the top of the hill, to see if his enemies were gone. Pulling out my spyglass, I looked, and saw plainly the place where they had been, but no sight of them or their canoes. It was plain they were gone, and had left their two comrades behind them, without any search for them.

I was not content with this discovery, but having now more courage, and more curiosity, I took my man Friday with me, giving him the sword in his hand, and the bow and arrows we had from the dead savages at his back, which I found he could use very easily. I also made him carry one gun for me. I carried two for myself, and away we marched to the place where these creatures had been. When I came to the place, my blood ran cold, and my heart sunk within me at the horror of the spectacle. Friday, by his signs, made me understand that they brought over four prisoners to feast upon. He indicated three of them were eaten up, and that he, pointing to himself, was to have been the fourth.

When we came back to our castle, I let him know I would give him some clothes, for he was stark naked. I gave him a pair of linen pants, which, with a little alteration, fitted him very well. Then I made him a goatskin jacket and a rabbit-fur cap. He was mightily pleased to see himself almost as well clothed as his

I gave him a pair of linen pants, which, with a little alteration, fitted him very well.

master. It is true, he went awkwardly in these things at first. Wearing pants was very awkward to him, and the sleeves of the coat bothered his shoulders and arms.

Never did a man have a more faithful, loving, sincere servant than Friday was to me. I was greatly delighted with him, and made it my business to teach him everything that was proper to make him useful, handy and helpful. The most important thing was to make him speak and understand me when I spoke. He was the best student that ever was, and so cheerful, hardworking and so pleased when he could understand me or make me understand him, that it was very pleasant to talk to him.

I set him to work to beating some grain, and sifting it in the manner I used to do. He soon understood how to do it, especially after he had seen what the meaning of it was, and that it was to make bread. After that I let him see me make my bread, and bake it too, and in a little time Friday was able to do all the work as well as I could do it myself.

Having two mouths to feed now instead of one, I needed to provide more ground for my harvest and plant a larger quantity of grain than I used to do. So I marked out a larger piece of land, and began the fence in the same manner as before, in which Friday not only worked very willingly and very hard, but did it very cheerfully. I told him what it was for, that it was for grain to make more bread, because he was now with me, and that I might have enough for him and myself too.

This was the pleasantest year of all the life I led in this place. Friday began to talk a great deal to me. I began now to have some use for my tongue again, which indeed I had very little use for before; that is to say, for speaking. Besides the pleasure of talking to him, I had a real satisfaction in the fellow himself. His simple honesty appeared to me more and more, and I began to love the creature. On his side, I believe he loved me.

Having taught him English so well that he could answer me almost any questions, I asked him whether the nation that he belonged to ever won their battles. He smiled and said, "Yes, yes, we always fight the better."

"You always fight the better," said I; "how was it that you were taken prisoner then, Friday?"

"My nation beat much, for all that," he replied.

"How beat?" I wondered. "If your nation beat them, how were you taken?"

"They more many than my nation in the place where me was. They take one, two, three and me. My nation overbeat them in the far place, where me no was. There my nation take one, two, great thousand," he said.

"But why," I continued, "did not your side recover you from the hands of your enemies then?"

Friday explained, "They run one, two, three and me, and make go in the canoe. My nation have no canoe that time."

"Well, Friday, what does your nation do with the men they take? Do they carry them away, and eat them, as these did?"

"Yes, my nation eats mans too, eat all up."

"Do they come here?"

"Yes, yes, they come here."

"Have you been here with them?"

Friday, pointing to the northwest side of the island, which, it seems, was their side, answered, "Yes, I been here."

By this I understood that my man Friday had been among the savages who used to come on shore on the farther part of the island. I asked him how far it was from our island to the shore, and whether canoes were not often lost. He told me there was no danger, no canoes ever got lost; but that after a little way out to the sea, there was a current, and a wind, always one way in the morning, the other in the afternoon.

I afterwards understood this current was controlled by the great outflow and inflow of the mighty Orinoco River, in the gulf of which river our island lay. The land which I could see to the west was, I found, the great island Trinidad.

I asked Friday a thousand questions about the country, the people who lived there, the sea, the coast and what nations were near. He told me all he knew.

I asked him once, after he had been with me a long time, who made him. He did not understand me at all, but thought I had asked who his father was. I took it by another route, and asked him who made the sea, the ground we walked on and the hills and woods. He told me it was one old Benamuckee, that lived beyond all. He could describe nothing of this great person but that he was very old; much older, he said, than the sea or the land, than the moon or the stars. I asked him then, if this old person had made all things, why did not all things worship him? He looked very serious, and with a perfect look of innocence, said "All things said O!" to him. I asked him if the people who die in this country went away anywhere. He said yes, they all went to Benamuckee. Then I asked him whether these men they eat went there too. He said yes.

After Friday and I got to know each other better, and he could understand almost all I said to him and speak fluently, though in broken English, I told him my own story, how I had lived there, and how long. I let him into the mystery of gunpowder and gunshot, and taught him how to shoot. I described to him Europe, and particularly England, which I came from. I told him how we lived, how we worshipped God, how we behaved to one another; and how we traded in ships to all parts of the world.

9

We Stop a Mutiny

I WAS NOW in my twenty-seventh year of living on this island. I kept the anniversary of my landing here with the same thankfulness to God for His mercies as at first. I had the feeling that my escape from this island would be soon, and that I should not be another year here. However, I went on with my farming, digging, planting, fencing, as usual. I gathered and dried my grapes, and did every necessary thing, as before.

After the rainy season, I was busy one morning, when I called to Friday and asked him to go to the seashore and see if he could find a turtle, a thing we generally got once a week, for the sake of the eggs as well as the meat. Friday had not been long gone when he came running back and flew over my outer wall. Before I had time to say a word, he cried out to me, "O Master! O Master! O sorrow! O bad!"

"What's the matter, Friday?"

"Master, master, they are come, they are come!"

I jumped up, and, not thinking of the danger, went out through my little grove, without my guns, which was not my custom to do. But I was surprised when, turning my eyes to the sea, I soon saw a boat a few

64

miles away, heading for shore, with a short sail, and the wind blowing pretty well to bring them in. I called to Friday and told him to lie low, that we did not know yet whether they were friends or enemies.

I went in to fetch my spyglass, to see what I could make of them. Having taken the ladder out, I climbed to the top of the hill to take my view without being seen.

I had hardly got up on the hill when my eye easily discovered a ship lying at anchor at about five miles distance from me, but not more than a few miles off shore. It appeared to be an English ship.

I cannot express the confusion I was in, though the joy of seeing a ship, and one I had reason to believe was manned by my own countrymen, and therefore friends, was such as I cannot describe. And yet I had some caution. I had to wonder why an English ship should be in that part of the world.

I watched the boat draw near the shore, as they looked for a creek for easier landing. However, as they did not come quite far enough, they did not see the little inlet where I used to land my rafts, but ran their boat on shore upon the beach, about a half a mile from me.

When they were on shore, I saw that they were indeed Englishmen, or at least most of them. There were in all eleven men, with three of them unarmed and tied up. When the first four or five of them jumped onto shore, they took those three out of the boat as prisoners.

Friday cried out to me in English, "O master! You see English mans eat prisoner as well as savage mans."

"Why," I said, "Friday, do you think they are going to eat them then?"

"Yes," said Friday, "they will eat them."

"No, no," I said, "I am afraid they will murder them, indeed, but you may be sure they will not eat them."

After I had observed the outrageous usage of the three men by the rude seamen, I observed the fellows run scattering about the land, as if they wanted to see the country. I observed that the other three men had been untied and were at liberty to go also where they pleased; but they sat down on the ground.

It was just at high water when these people came on shore, and while talking and rambling about the island, they had carelessly stayed till the tide was gone, and now their boat was grounded. It would be at least ten hours before the boat could be floated again, and by that time it would be dark.

In the meantime I fitted myself up for a battle. I ordered Friday also to load himself with guns. I took two bird guns and I gave him three muskets. I had my goatskin coat on, with the large cap, a sword by my side, two pistols in my belt, and a gun upon each shoulder.

I had planned not to make any move till it was dark. But about two o'clock, I found that they were all in the woods and fallen asleep. The three hostages, worried about their fate, did not sleep, but were sitting under the shelter of a large tree, out of sight of the rest.

I resolved to go to them and learn something of their condition. Immediately I set out towards them, my man Friday at a good distance behind me. Before any of them saw me, I called aloud to them, "What are you, gentlemen?"

They started at my words, but were more surprised by my appearance. I saw that they were about to run away, so I said to them: "Gentlemen, do not be surprised by me. I may be your friend."

One of them said, "Am I talking to God, or man? Is it a real man, or an angel?"

"I am a man," I said, "an Englishman, who would like to help you. I have one servant only. We have guns and ammunition. Tell us, can we help you? What is your story?"

"Our story," said he, "sir, is too long to tell you, while our murderers are so near. But in short, sir, I was commander of that ship. My men have mutinied against me, they have hardly held themselves back from killing me. Instead they have set me on shore in this desolate place, with these two men with me, one my mate, the other a passenger, where we expect to die."

"Have the brutes any guns?" I asked.

He answered that they had only two guns, one of which they left in the boat.

"Shall we take them as prisoners?" I asked.

He told me there were two desperate villains among

I resolved to go to them and learn something of their
condition.

them, but that if those two were captured, he believed all the rest would return to their duty.

"Sir," said I, "if I help you to escape, are you willing to make pledges to me?"

He said he knew what I would ask, and that if the ship were recovered, he would be at my command. If it were not recovered, he declared he would live and die with me. The other two men said the same.

"Well, then," I said, "here are three muskets for you, with gunpowder and bullets."

He took the musket, and with his two men approached the slumbering mutineers. One of the seamen woke up and cried out. The captain's two men fired their guns and killed one man and wounded another. The others gave up and begged for mercy. The captain told them he would spare their lives, if they would swear to be faithful to him in recovering the ship and afterwards sailing her back to Jamaica, from where they had come. They promised, and he believed them, which I was not against, only I asked the captain to keep them bound hand and foot while they were upon the island.

I now told the captain my whole history, which amazed him. He was particularly amazed at the way I had furnished myself with goods and guns. Indeed, as my story is a whole collection of wonders, it affected him deeply. I then took him and his two men into my castle, where I fed them and gave them drink, and showed them my many works. All I showed them, all I said to them, was perfectly amazing. Above all, the

captain admired my fort, and how well I had hidden
my retreat with a grove of trees.

At present, however, our business was to consider
how to recover the ship. He told me he did not know
what to do, that there were still twenty-six men on
board who would fight us.

We went back to the shore and saw, with the use of
the spyglass, that the mutineers on board ship were
launching another boat for the island. We found, as
they approached, that there were ten men in the boat,
and that they had guns with them.

We hid and watched them come on shore, hauling
the boat up after them. After they looked around for a
while, they let out two or three great shouts, helloing
with all their might, to try to get their companions to
hear. They fired off guns as a signal, but there was no
response. They were so surprised, they went back to
their boat and launched it to return to the ship. But
they were not far off before they returned to the shore.
This time they left three men in the boat, and seven
got out to search the island for their mates.

After the seven were amongst the woods, we surprised the men in the boat, and captured it. By the
time the other seven returned to the shore from the
woods, it was night.

We came upon the mutineers in the dark, so that
they could not see us. After a short fight in which two
of the mutineers were killed, we forced the others to
surrender.

Our next work was to think of how to seize the

ship. Our captives, in order to try to regain the captain's sympathy and thus make their case before a judge in Jamaica go easier, agreed to help us. The captain put himself at the head of one boat, and his passenger the captain of the other, with four men in each. They rowed out to the ship and arrived about midnight. As soon as they came within call of the ship, he made one of the captive mutineers hail them and tell them they had brought off the first men who had gone over, and the boat. But then, upon entering the ship, the captain and his mate knocked down two mutineers aboard ship, and began locking down the hatches to keep the other mutineers below the deck. When this was done, and all safe upon deck, the captain ordered the mate with three good men to break into the cabin where the leader of the muti- neers was hiding. As they borke down the door, guns went off, and though the captain's mate was wounded, he continued his charge and shot dead the chief mutineer. The rest of the mutineers surrendered, and no more lives were lost.

As soon as the ship was thus recovered, the captain ordered seven guns to be fired, which was the signal agreed upon with me, to give me notice of his success. Having heard the signal, I went to sleep. In the morning I awoke, hearing the captain's voice from atop the hill near my castle. He came to me, hugged me, and told me, "My dear friend, there's your ship, for she is all yours, and so are we and all that belong to her."

At first, for some time, I was not able to answer him one word. He said a thousand kind things to me, to calm me and bring me around. But such was the flood of joy in my heart that I was confused. At last I broke out into tears, and a little while after I was able to speak. I told him that I saw him as my rescuer.

From the ship he brought me presents: wine, tobacco, pork, peas, biscuits, sugar, flour, lemons and an abundance of other things. But even more useful to me, he brought me six clean new shirts, two pairs of gloves, one pair of shoes, a hat, one pair of stockings and a very good suit of clothes of his own, which had been worn very little. He clothed me from head to foot.

Some time after this the boat was ordered on shore, the tide being up. When Friday and I took leave of this island, I carried on board for souvenirs the large goatskin cap I had made, my umbrella, and one of my parrots. And thus I left the island, the 19th of December, in the year 1686, after I had been upon it twenty-eight years, two months and nineteen days.

In this vessel, after a long voyage, I arrived in England the 11th of June, in the year 1687, having been thirty-five years absent.

When I came to England, I was a perfect stranger, as if I had never been known there. I went down to Yorkshire. My father and my mother, however, and all my family were dead except two sisters and two of the children of one of my brothers.

The owners of the ship, after the captain told them